GRAHAM GREENE

THE THIRD MAN

Originally edited by Aage Salling and Erik Hvid
Revised by Robert Dewsnap 1991
Illustrations by Jørgen Hedegaard 1993

EASY READERS
ER

The vocabulary is based on
Michael West: A General Service List of
English Words, revised & enlarged edition 1953
Pacemaker Core Vocabulary, 1975
Salling/Hvid: English-Danish Basic Dictionary, 1970
J. A. van Ek: The Threshold Level for Modern Language
Learning in Schools, 1976

Cover layout: Mette Plesner

ISBN Denmark 87-11-08808-7

Printed in Denmark by
Sangill Bogtryk & offset, Holme Olstrup

GRAHAM GREENE
(1904–1991)

was born at Berkhamsted in Hertfordshire, where his father was headmaster of the public school. He counts as one of the greatest British prose writers of the twentieth century. His capacity for narrative recalls that of R. L. Stevenson, his father's cousin, but he never writes a story for its own sake; over and above the plot something else happens which is of far greater importance than the events which make up the plot. He wants to show how inevitably and mercilessly the choice between good and evil comes into the life of every man. Flight is often the theme he chooses to deprive his characters of everything which can obscure the issue, and with deep psychological insight Greene shows us the result in persons of different turns of mind. His style is clear, his symbols well chosen, and his language carefully phrased to express exactly what he wants to say.

The Third Man, Graham Greene has said, was never intended to be more than the raw material for a film. The film was directed by Carol Reed in 1950, Orson Welles played the part of Harry Lime, and the theme tune by Anton Karas has taken on a life of its own outside the film.

Some other books by Graham Greene:
Stamboul Train (1932; US title, Orient Express), A Gun for Sale (1936; US title, This Gun For Hire, filmed 1942), Brighton Rock (1938, filmed 1948), The Confidential Agent (1939, filmed 1945), The Power and the Glory (1940, filmed 1962), The Ministry of Fear (1943, filmed 1945), The Heart of the Matter (1948), The End of the Affair (1951), The Quiet American (1955), Our Man in Havana (1958, filmed 1959), A Burnt-Out Case (1961), The Pleasure Dome (1972), The Honorary Consul (1973), The Human Factor (1978), Doctor Fischer of Geneva or The Bomb Party (1980), Monsignor Quixote (1982), Getting to Know the General (1984), The Tenth Man (1985), The Captain and the Enemy (1988).
He has also written plays, essays, travel books, children's books, short stories, and two volumes of autobiography, A Sort of Life (1971) and Ways of Escape (1980).

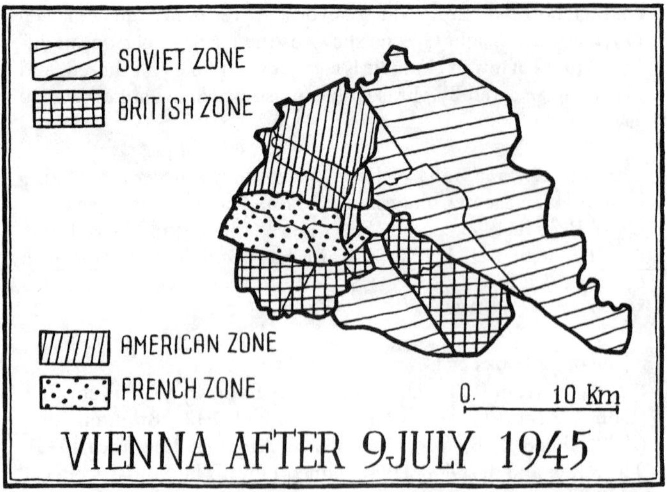
SOVIET ZONE
BRITISH ZONE
AMERICAN ZONE
FRENCH ZONE
0 10 Km
VIENNA AFTER 9JULY 1945

1

When I saw Rollo Martins first, I made this note on him for my police *files*: "Normally a happy fool. Drinks too much, and looks at women. Has never really grown up, and perhaps that is why he loved Lime as a hero."

I met Rollo Martins first at Harry Lime's *funeral*. It was February, and the *grave-diggers* had been forced to use electric *drills* to open the frozen ground in Vienna's Central *Cemetery*. It was as if nature were refusing to accept Lime, but we got him in at last and laid the earth

Harry Lime's funeral in Vienna's Central Cemetery

---

file (here), papers with information about a certain person
grave-diggers, *drill*, see picture, page 6

back on him in blocks. Then Rollo Martins walked away as though his long legs wanted to run, and the tears of a boy ran down his thirty-five-year-old face. Rollo Martins believed in friendship. So the things that happened later were a worse shock to him than they would have been to you or me.

If you are to understand this sad and strange story, you must have an idea at least of the background. The city of Vienna is divided up in *zones* among the Four Powers: the Russian, the British, the American and the French zones. In the centre lies the Inner City, under the control of all Four Powers. In this Inner City each power in turn, for a month at a time, is in charge and takes care of things. I am too young to remember the old Vienna with its Strauss music and its easy charm. I only know the Prater as a park in the Russian zone destroyed by *the war*, Sacher's as a hotel for passing English officers, and the Kärntnerstrasse as a street of ruins. To me, Vienna is simply a city of ruins which turned that February into blocks of snow and ice.

zone, see picture, page 4
the war, the Second World War, 1939–45

2

A British subject can still travel – if he takes with him only five pounds, which he is forbidden to spend abroad; but Rollo Martins was only allowed to enter Austria because he had received an invitation from Lime.

Lime worked at the International *Refugee* Office. He wanted Martins to write something about the refugees, and he had promised to pay Martins' expenses. Though this was not Martins' *line* he had agreed to do so. His usual line was the writing of cheap *Westerns* under the name of Buck Dexter. He had many readers but did not make much money from the books.

A strange thing had happened at Frankfurt, where the *plane* from London stopped for an hour. Martins was eating a hamburger in the American cafeteria when a newspaperman came up to his table.

"You Mr Dexter?" he asked.

"Yes," Martins said.

"Would you like to say something? I represent the

plane

---

refugees, people who have had to leave their homes and go to other countries because of the war

line, kind of work

Western, story about cowboys etc in the West of the U.S.A.

American newspaper here. We'd like to know what you think of Frankfurt."

"I only arrived ten minutes ago."

"All right," the man said. "What about your views on the American *novel*?"

"I don't read novels," Martins said.

The man pointed at a small grey-haired man at another table. "Do you know if that's Carey?"

"No. What Carey?

"J G Carey, of course."

"I've never heard of him."

"You novelists live out of the world." The man walked across the room to meet the great Carey, but Martins could not help feeling proud that the other had spoken of him as a novelist. That carried him over the *disappointment* when Lime was not there to meet him at the airport.

Nor was there any Lime to meet him at the Hotel Astoria, nor any message – only one for Mr Dexter, from someone he had never heard of called Crabbin. "We expected you on tomorrow's plane. Please stay where you are. Coming round. Hotel room reserved." But Rollo was not the kind of man who stayed around. If you stayed in a hotel, sooner or later something happened, and Rollo Martins wanted none of that.

He had been given Lime's address and he was not very willing to meet the man called Crabbin; a mistake must have been made. So Martins drove straight away to the building in the British zone. He kept the taxi

---

novel, long story that fills a book
disappointment, feeling of sadness that something expected has not happened

waiting while he went up to the third floor.

Martins hadn't got to the second floor before he knew that he would not find Lime there. It was as if he would not find Lime anywhere in Vienna, and, as he reached the third floor and saw the big black *bow* over the door *handle*, anywhere in the world at all.

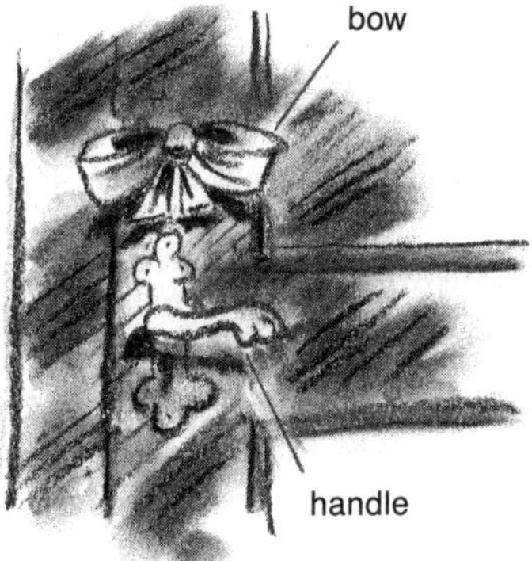

Of course it might be a cook who had died, a *housekeeper*, anybody but Harry Lime; but he knew – he had known twenty stairs down – that Lime, the Lime he had looked up to now for twenty years, since their first meeting in a school corridor, was gone. Martins wasn't wrong. After he had rung the bell five or six times, a small man put his head out from another flat and told him, "It's no use. There's nobody there. He's dead."

"Herr Lime?"

"Herr Lime, of course."

Martins said to me later, "At first it didn't mean a thing. It was just a bit of information, like what you see in a newspaper. I said to him, 'When did it happen? How?'

---

housekeeper, woman taking care of the flat

"He was run over by a car," the man said. "Last Thursday." And then, as if it were really none of his business, "They're burying him this afternoon. You've just missed them."

"Them?"

"Oh, a couple of friends and the *coffin*."

"Wasn't he in hospital?"

"There was no sense in taking him to hospital. He was killed on his own doorstep. The car struck him on his shoulder and *bowled* him *over* like a rabbit."

It was only then, Martins told me, when the man used the word "rabbit", that the dead Harry Lime came alive. Harry Lime became the boy with the gun in a field near the school, going after rabbits; a boy saying to Martins, "Shoot, you fool, shoot! There," and the rabbit crept painfully home, wounded by Martins' shot.

"Where are they burying him?" he asked the stranger.

"In the Central Cemetery. They'll have a hard time of it in this frost."

He had no idea how to pay for his taxi, but he drove straight out of town into the British zone where the Central Cemetery lay. One passed through the Russian and American zones to reach it. The road ran along the high wall of the cemetery, and for a mile on the other side was the endless line of *gravestones*.

It was just by chance that he reached the funeral in

coffin, wooden box for the dead body
bowl over, knock over
gravestone, see picture, page 5

jeep

time. A small group was gathered, a priest had just spoken, and a coffin was on the point of being lowered into the ground. Two men stood at the grave. A girl stood a little way away with her hands over her face. I stood a little further away by another grave, glad to see the last of Lime – just a man in a raincoat I was to Martins. He came up to me and said, "Could you tell me who they are burying?"

"A fellow called Lime," I said, and was surprised to see the tears start to this stranger's eyes; he did not look like a man to whom tears came easily.

Martins stood there, till the end, close beside me. As soon as the affair was over he walked away on his long legs, back to his taxi. He did not try to speak to anyone, and the tears were now really running, at any rate the few drops that can come to the eyes of a man at our age.

I followed Martins. I knew the other three. I wanted to know the stranger. I caught him up by his taxi and said, “I haven’t any transport. May I share your taxi into town?”

“Of course,” he said. I knew that the driver of my *jeep* would see me as we came out and follow us. As we drove away I noticed that Martins never looked behind.

“I said, “My name is Calloway.”

“Martins,” he said.

“You were a friend of Lime?”

“Yes.” Few people in the last week would have been willing to say that.

“Been here long?”

“I only came this afternoon from England. Harry had asked me to stay with him. I hadn’t heard.”

“Bit of a shock?”

“Look here,” he said. “I badly want a drink, but I haven’t any Austrian money – only five pounds from England. I’d be very happy if you would buy me one.”

It was my turn to say “Of course”. I thought for a moment and told the driver the name of a small bar in the Kärntnerstrasse. I didn’t think Martins would want to be seen for a while in a busy British bar full of officers and their wives. This bar seldom had more than one couple in it at a time. The bar only had one drink – a sweet chocolate liqueur – but it seemed to me that Martins did not mind any drink so long as it made him forget. We had a whole room to ourselves; the waiter, who knew me, left us alone.

Martins said, over his second drink, “I’m sorry, but he was the best friend I ever had.”

---

jeep, see picture, page 11

I wanted to make Martins a little angry – one learns a lot that way. So I said, "That sounds like a cheap short novel."

He said quickly, "I write cheap short novels."

I said, "Tell me about yourself – and Lime."

"Look here," he said. "I badly need another drink, but I can't keep on asking a stranger. Could you change me a pound into Austrian money?"

"Never mind that," I said and called the waiter. "You can buy me a drink when I come to London. You were going to tell me how you met Lime?"

He looked at his glass, and turned it this way and that. He said, "It was a long time ago. I don't suppose anyone knows Harry the way I do," and I thought of all the things my office knew about Lime.

"How long?"

"Twenty years – or a bit more. I met him when I was a new boy at school. I can see the place. I can hear the bell ringing. He was a year older and knew everything about the school. He taught me a lot of things."

He drank a little and then turned the glass again as if to see more clearly what there was to see. He said, "It's funny. I can't remember meeting any woman quite as well."

"Was he clever at school?"

"Not the way they wanted him to be. But what things he did think up! I was far better at things like History and English than Harry, but I was no good when it came to carrying out his plans." Martins laughed: he was already beginning, with the help of drink and talk, to throw off the shock of the death. He said, "I was always the one who got caught."

I said, "That was nice for Lime."

"What do you mean?" he asked angrily.

"Well, wasn't it?"

"That was my fault, not his. He could have found someone cleverer." Certainly, I thought.

"When did you see him last?"

"Oh, he was in London six months ago for a medical conference. You know he was a doctor, though he never *practised*. That was just like him. He just wanted to see if he could do a thing, and then he lost interest. But he often said it might be useful later." And that too was true. It was strange: the Lime that Martins knew was very like the Lime I knew; it was only that Martins looked at him in a different light.

Martins said, "One of the things I liked about Harry was his humour." He gave a broad smile which made him look five years younger.

He whistled a tune

He *whistled a tune* – I thought I knew it. "I always remember that. I saw Harry write it. Just in a few minutes on a piece of paper. That was what he always whistled when he was thinking." Martins whistled the tune again, and I knew then who had written it – of course it wasn't Harry. I nearly told him so, but why should I? He looked into his glass, drank what was left, and said, "It's sad to think of him dying like that."

---

practise, work (as a doctor)

"It was the best thing that ever happened to him," I said.

He did not understand at once. "The best thing?"

"Yes."

"You mean there wasn't any pain?"

"He was lucky in that way, too."

It was my tone of voice, and not my words that caught Martins' attention. He asked – I could see his right hand close and harden – "What do you mean?"

I moved my chair away from him, and said, "I mean, we know all about him at police *headquarters*. He would have gone to prison for a long time – if this had not happened."

"What for?"

"He was the worst *racketeer* who ever came to this city." I could see him measure the distance between us and decide that he could not reach me from where he sat.

"You're a policeman?" he said.

"Yes."

"I have always hated policemen. They are usually stupid."

"Is that the kind of book you write?"

I could see him moving his chair to block my way out. I caught the waiter's eye and he knew what I meant – there's an advantage in always using the same bar for interviews.

Martins said with a smile, "I write about American policemen."

"Been in America?"

---

headquarters, central office
racketeer, person making money in a dishonest way

"No. Why do you ask?"

"Just interest."

"Because you think that if Harry was a racketeer, I must be one too. We always worked together."

"I daresay he wanted to bring you into the *racket* too. Quite possibly he meant to *give you the baby to hold*. That was his method at school – you told me, didn't you?"

"That's just like a policeman, to put the blame on a dead man. You're a real policeman, I suppose?"

"Yes, Scotland Yard, but they've put me into a *colonel*'s uniform when I'm on duty."

He was between me and the door now. "Why don't you policemen catch a few murderers for a change?"

"Well, you could say that murder was part of his racket."

He pushed the table over with one hand and struck at me with the other. Before he could try again, my driver had his arms round him.

"Be quiet, can't you, sir?" my driver said.

"Listen, Callaghan, or whatever your name is ..."

"Calloway, I'm English, not Irish."

"I'm going to make you look the biggest fool in Vienna," said Martins. "There is one dead man you aren't going put the blame on."

"I see. You're going to find me the real criminal? It sounds like one of your stories."

"You can let me go, Callaghan. I would rather let you look the fool you are than give you a black eye. But

---

give you the baby to hold, run away and leave you in trouble
colonel, army officer ranking below general
racket, a racketeer's business

when I've finished with you, you'll leave Vienna."

I took a couple of pounds' worth of *bafs* and stuck them in his pocket. "These will be enough for tonight," I said. "And I'll make sure they keep a seat for you on tomorrow's London plane."

"You can't make me leave. My papers are in order."

"Yes, but you need money here, and you can't change your pounds. Let him go, Paine."

"Thanks for the drinks."

"That's all right. I might come and see you off tomorrow."

"I shouldn't waste your time. I won't be there."

"Paine here will show you the way to Sacher's. You can get a bed and dinner there. I'll arrange it."

He stepped to one side and struck at me, and I fell against the table. Before he could try again, Paine hit him on the nose. I said, "I thought you had promised not to fight."

He wiped some of the blood away from his face and said, "Oh, no, I said I would rather make you a fool. I didn't say that I wouldn't give you a black eye."

I had had a long day and was tired of Rollo Martins. When I left the bar, I heard Paine say to the man he had just knocked down, "This way, sir. It's only just round the corner."

---

bafs, BAFVs, British Armed Forces Vouchers: tickets given after the Second World War to British military people abroad, to stop them using British money on the local black market

3

What happened next I didn't hear from Paine but from Martins a long time afterwards, and it did prove me to be a fool.

Paine took Martins to the *porter's desk* and explained there, "This gentleman came in on the plane from London. Colonel Calloway says he is to have a room," and left.

"Had you already got a reservation, sir?" the porter asked.

"No. No, I don't think so," Martins said.

"I thought perhaps you might be Mr Dexter. We had a room reserved for a week for Mr Dexter."

Martins said, "Oh, I am Mr Dexter." He told me later that he thought perhaps Lime had got him a room in that name. A voice said at his side, "I'm so sorry you were not met at the plane, Mr Dexter. My name's

Crabbin. Our Institute thought that you were going to Stockholm, not to Vienna. Then one of our fellows heard that you were on the plane in Frankfurt. You got my note?"

Martins held his handkerchief to his mouth and said, "Yes. Yes."

"May I say at once, Mr Dexter, how happy I am to meet you?"

"Good of you."

"Ever since I was a boy, I have thought you the greatest novelist of our time."

Martins looked angrily at Mr Crabbin.

"You have many readers in Austria, Mr Dexter."

Martins was thinking hard. "Did you say – room for a week?"

"Yes."

"Very kind of you."

"Mr Schmidt here, the porter, will give you tickets every day, for your meals. But I think you will need some pocket money. We'll fix that. Tomorrow we thought you would like a quiet day to look around."

"Yes."

"Then the day after tomorrow, in the evening, there is a discussion – on today's English novel. We thought you would like to say a few words."

At that moment Martins was prepared to do anything. He wanted Mr Crabbin to leave him alone, and he also wanted a free room and food for a week. He said, "Of course, of course," into his handkerchief.

"Excuse me, Mr Dexter, have you got a bad tooth? I know a very good *dentist*."

---

dentist, doctor who takes care of people's teeth

"No. Somebody hit me, that's all."

"Good God! Were they trying to rob you?"

"No, it was a soldier. We were fighting."

Crabbin was so surprised that he did not know what to say. Martins couldn't understand why. That was because he, writing under the name of Buck Dexter, had never read the work of the great English novelist Benjamin Dexter: he hadn't even heard of him. I very much like Dexter's novels, so I could understand Crabbin's surprise: no one would expect that English novelist to get into a fight.

"Have you heard of Harry Lime?" Martins asked.

"Yes," said Crabbin carefully, "but I didn't really know him."

"I did. He was my best friend."

"A friend of his - an *actress*, you know - is learning English at our Institute. He came once or twice to fetch her."

"Young or old?"

"Oh, young, very young. Not a good actress in my opinion."

Martins remembered the girl by the grave with her hands over her face. He said, "I would like to meet any friend of Harry's. Is she Austrian?"

"She says she is, but I think she is Hungarian. I should not be surprised if Lime helped her with her papers. She calls herself Schmidt. Anna Schmidt."

Martins felt he had got all he could from Crabbin. He said he was tired after a long day, promised to ring Crabbin in the morning, accepted ten pounds' worth of bafs, and went to his room. It seemed to him that

---

actress, girl or woman who acts on the *stage* or in films

an actress on the stage

he was making money quickly – twelve pounds in less than an hour.

He **was** tired; he realized that when he lay down on his bed in his boots. Within a minute he was fast asleep. He dreamed of Harry Lime, and of being pleased to meet him. He woke suddenly to hear the telephone ringing by his bed.

A voice said, "Is that Mr Rollo Martins?"

"Yes." It was a change to be himself and not Dexter.

"You wouldn't know me," the voice said, "but I was a friend of Harry Lime."

It was a change too to hear anyone say that he was a friend of Harry Lime. Martins said, "I'll be glad to meet you."

"I'm just round the corner at the Old Vienna."

"Couldn't we meet tomorrow? I've had a pretty awful day with one thing and another."

"Harry asked me to see that you were all right. I was with him when he died."

"I thought –" Rollo Martins said, and then stopped. He had been going to say, "I thought he died immediately," but he thought better of it. He said instead, "You haven't told me your name."

"Kurtz," the voice said. "I would come round to you, only, you know, Austrians are not allowed in Sacher's."

"Perhaps we could meet at the Old Vienna in the morning."

"Certainly," the voice said, "if you are **quite** sure that you are all right till then?"

"How do you mean?"

"Harry had it on his mind that you'd have no money."

Rollo Martins lay back on his bed with the *receiver* to his ear and thought, "Come to Vienna to make money." This was the third stranger to offer him money in less than five hours. He said, "I can carry on till I see you."

"Shall we say eleven, then, at the Old Vienna in the Kärntnerstrasse? I'll be in a brown suit and I'll carry one of your books."

"That's fine. How did you get hold of the book?"

"Harry gave it to me."

Martins said good night and rang off. He wondered about Harry. Harry had been able to think of so many things before he died. Yet he had not told anyone to send a telegram to stop him coming from England. Why was that? Hadn't Callaghan said that Lime had died immediately – or without pain, was it? Or had he himself put the words into Callaghan's mouth? It was

then that the idea first came to Martins that there was something wrong about Lime's death, something the police had been too stupid to discover. He tried to discover it himself with the help of two cigarettes, but he fell asleep without his dinner and without discovering anything. It had been a long day, but not quite long enough for that.

4

"What I didn't like about him," Martins told me, "was his *toupée*. It was flat and yellow, with the hair cut straight at the back and not fitting close. There must be something false about a man who wears a toupée."

Martins and I were sitting in the Old Vienna at the table he had occupied that first morning with Kurtz. When Martins made that remark about the toupée, I saw his eyes suddenly catch something. It was a girl – just like any other girl, I thought, going by in the snow outside.

"Something pretty?" I asked.

"No. You know, Calloway, a time comes in a man's life when he gives up all that sort of thing . . ."

"I see. I thought you were looking at a girl."

"I was. But only because she reminded me for a moment of Anna – Anna Schmidt."

"Who is she? Isn't she a girl?"

"Oh, yes, in a way."

"What do you mean, in a way?"

"She was Harry's girl."

"You were telling me about Kurtz," I said.

It appeared that Kurtz was sitting there, making a great show of reading The Lone Rider of Santa Fé. When Martins sat down at his table Kurtz said, "It's wonderful how you keep the *tension*."

"Tension?"

---

toupée, false hair
tension, excitement while waiting to see what will happen

"Yes. At the end of each chapter one is left to guess . . ."

"So you were a friend of Harry's," Martins said.

"I think his best," but Kurtz added after a short pause, "except you, of course."

"Tell me how he died."

"I was with him. We came out together from the door of his flat, and Harry saw a friend he knew across the road – an American called Cooler. Harry waved to Cooler and started across the road to him when a jeep came round the corner very fast and bowled him over. It was Harry's fault – not the driver's."

"Somebody told me he died immediately."

"I wish he had. He died before the *ambulance* could reach us, though."

"He could speak, then?"

"Yes."

"What did he say?"

"I can't remember the exact words, Rollo – I may call you Rollo, mayn't I? He always called you that to us. – He very much wanted me to look after you when you arrived. Get your return ticket for you.“

"But why didn't you send a telegram to stop me?"

"We did, but it must have missed you."

"There was an *inquest*?"

"Of course."

"Did you know that the police think Harry was mixed up in some racket?"

---

ambulance, large white car to take people who are sick or hurt to hospital

inquest, official meeting held by a doctor and others to find the cause of death

"No. But everyone in Vienna is. We all sell cigarettes and exchange *schillings* for bafs and that kind of thing."

"The police meant something worse than that."

"They get funny ideas sometimes."

"I'm going to stay here till I prove them wrong."

Kurtz turned his head sharply. He said, "I don't see what you can do."

"I'm going to start working back from his death. You

---

schillings, (German *Schillinge*), Austrian money

were there, and this man Cooler, and the driver. You can give me their addresses."

"I don't know the driver's address."

"I can get it from the police. And then there's Harry's girl ..."

Kurtz said, "It will be hard on her."

"I don't care about her, only about Harry."

"What racket are the police thinking of, exactly? Do you know?"

"No."

"Have you thought," said Kurtz, "that you might find something – well, something unpleasant, and that it will take time – and money?"

"I've got time, and you were going to lend me some money, weren't you?"

"I'm not a rich man," Kurtz said. "I promised Harry to see you were all right and that you got your plane back ..."

"You needn't worry about the money. But I'm sure that there's something strange about Harry's death."

It was a shot in the dark, but already Martins' instinct told him him that something was wrong.

Kurtz had a cup of coffee half-way to his lips and Martins watched him. Kurtz drank a little, then put down the cup and said, "How do you mean – strange?"

"There was a dead body," said Martins. "That was useful for the police. But wouldn't it have been equally useful, perhaps, for the real racketeers?"

Kurtz had drunk his coffee as though nothing had been said. "Well," he said, "I don't believe there's anything to find. But just ask me for any help you want."

"I want Cooler's address."

"Certainly. I'll write it down for you. Here it is.

Cooler lives in the American zone."

"And your address?"

"It's there too. I'm unlucky enough to be in the Russian zone. But I still think you are not wise."

He picked up The Lone Rider. "I'm so proud to have met you. A master of tension," and with one hand on the toupée, and the other passing over his mouth, he brushed a smile from his face as though it had never been.

* * *

5

Martins sat on a hard chair just inside the Josefstadt Theatre. He had sent up his *card* to Anna Schmidt, marking it "a friend of Harry's."

It was cold, so that Martins rose and walked up and down under the little windows.

He had had time to think: he was calm now. When a light went out in one of the windows and an actress came down, he didn't even turn to take a look. He thought: Kurtz is right, they are all right, they are all right, I am a fool. I'll just have a word with Anna Schmidt, and then I'll pack and go. He had quite forgotten, he told me, Mr Crabbin.

A voice over his head called "Mr Martins" and he looked up at the face. It wasn't a beautiful face, just an honest face: dark hair and dark eyes, perhaps brown, and a large mouth which didn't try to charm. She said, "Will you come up, please? The second door on the right."

There are some people, Martins explained to me, whom you know at once to be friends. "That was Anna," he said.

There was a *kettle* on the gas ring. She said, "Would you like a cup of tea? Someone sent me a *packet* last week."

"I'd like a cup," he said, but if there was one thing he hated it was tea. He watched her while she made it – made it, of course, all wrong: the water was not hot, too few leaves. She said, "I never quite understand why English people like tea."

He drank it quickly like medicine. He said, "I

wanted very much to see you. About Harry."

This was the terrible moment; he could see her mouth move.

"Yes?"

"I had known him for twenty years. I was his friend. We were at school together, you know, and after that – we met several times a year . . ."

She said, "When I got your card, I couldn't say no. But there's nothing really for us to talk about, is there? – Nothing."

"I wanted to hear –"

"He's dead. That's the end. Everything's over, finished. What's the good of talking?"

"We both loved him."

"I don't know. You can't know a thing like that – afterwards. I don't know anything any more except –"

"Except?"

"That I want to be dead too."

Martins told me, "Then I nearly went away. But instead I asked her one question, 'Do you know a man called Cooler?'"

"An American?" she asked. "I think that was the man who brought me some money when Harry died. I didn't want to take it, but he said Harry had worried about me – at the last moment."

"So he didn't die immediately?"

"Oh, no."

Martins said to me, "I began to wonder why I had got that idea so firmly into my head – that Harry had died immediately. And then I thought: it was only the man in the flat who told me so – no one else. I said to her, 'He must have been very clear in his head at the end – because he remembered about me too. That seems to show that there wasn't really any pain.'"

"That's what I tell myself all the time."

"Did you see the doctor?"

"Once. Harry sent me to him. He was Harry's own doctor. He lived nearby, you see."

Martins suddenly seemed to see before him a desert place, a body on the ground, and a group of birds gathered. But the picture was gone in a moment, and he thought how strange that they were all there, just at that moment, all Harry's friends – Kurtz, the doctor, this man Cooler; only the two people who loved him seemed to have been missing. Martins said, "And the driver? Did you hear what he said at the inquest?"

"It wasn't his fault. I've often heard Harry say what a careful driver he was."

"The driver knew Harry too?" Another bird flew down and joined the others round the silent figure on the sand who lay face down. Now he could tell it was Harry, by the clothes, lying like a boy asleep in the grass on a hot summer day.

Somebody called outside the window. "*Fräulein* Schmidt."

She said, "They don't like one to stay too long."

Martins said, "The police say they were going to arrest Harry. They thought he was in a racket."

"Everybody is in a racket."

"I don't believe he was in anything serious."

"No," she agreed.

"Do you know a man called Kurtz?"

"I don't think so."

"He wears a toupée."

Fräulein (German), Miss

"Oh."

His remark had hit the spot, he could tell that. He said, "Don't you think that it was strange they were all there – at the death? Everybody knew Harry. Even the driver, the doctor . . ."

She said with hopeless calm, "I've wondered that too. I wondered whether they had murdered him, but what's the use of wondering?"

"I'm going to get those *bastards*," Martins said.

"It won't do any good –"

"Fräulein Schmidt," the voice called again.

"I'll walk with you a bit of the way."

They left the theatre. Anna said, "It's better to give up and forget."

"Will you give me the doctor's address?"

They stood still while she wrote it down for him.

"And yours too?"

"Why do you want that?"

"I might have news for you."

"There isn't any news that would do any good now."

---

bastards, evil men. (A bastard is really a man whose mother was not married to his father)

6

An amateur detective has the advantage over the professional that he doesn't work certain set hours. Rollo Martins did as much work in one day as one of my men would have done in two. And he had this advantage, too, that he was Harry's friend.

Dr Winkler was at home. Perhaps he would not have been at home to a police officer. Again Martins had written on his card: A friend of Harry Lime's.

Dr Winkler's waiting-room reminded Martins of an *antique shop*. There were more *crucifixes* than he could count, and most of them about three hundred years old. There were *statues*. There were little bits of bone marked with the names of *saints* and set in *oval frames*. What a strange thing for Saint Susanna's finger-bone to come to rest in Dr Winkler's waiting-room. Martins heard a *sneeze* behind him.

Dr Winkler was the cleanest doctor Martins had ever seen. He was very small and neat and dressed in black. He sneezed again: perhaps he was cold because he was so clean. He said, "Mr Martins?"

Martins answered, "Dr Winkle?"

"Dr Winkler."

"You've got an interesting collection here."

"Yes."

---

antique shop, shop selling very old furniture etc
crucifix, statue, see picture, page 34
saint, very holy person, well known in church history
oval frame, see picture, page 34
sneeze, sudden outburst of air through the nose, the sign that someone has a cold

oval frame
crucifix
statue

"These saints' bones . . ."

"The bones of chickens and rabbits." Dr Winkler took a large white handkerchief and blew his nose carefully twice. You expected him to throw away the handkerchief after one use. "Would you mind, Mr Martins, telling me what I can do for you? I have a patient waiting."

"We were both friends of Harry Lime."

"I was his doctor."

"I arrived too late for the inquest. Harry had invited me to come out here and help him in something. I don't know quite what. I didn't hear of his death till I arrived."

"Very sad," said Dr Winkler.

"Of course I want to hear all I can."

"There is nothing I can tell you that you don't know. He was knocked over by a car. He was dead when I arrived."

"You are quite certain that it was an accident?"

Dr Winkler put out a hand and touched a crucifix. "I was not there. I only know what he died of."

Martins said, "The police thought he was in a very serious racket. It seemed to me that he might have been murdered – or even killed himself."

"I could not say," Dr Winkler said.

"Do you know a man called Cooler?"

"I don't think so."

"He was there when Harry was killed."

"Then of course I have met him. He wears a toupée."

"That was Kurtz."

Dr Winkler was not only the cleanest, he was also the most careful doctor that Martins had ever met. His statements were so short that you felt they must be true. He said, "There was a second man there."

"Had you been Harry's doctor for long?"

"For about a year."

"Well, it's good of you to have seen me." Dr Winkler bowed. Martins said, "I mustn't keep you from your patients any longer." He turned away from the doctor. "That's a strange crucifix," he said. "Why are the arms above the head?"

"It is *Jansenist*, and in their view He died only for the chosen few."

Jansenist, belonging to a group in the Roman Catholic Church that believes the natural human will is unable to do good

7

As I see it, it would still have been possible, at this moment, for Rollo Martins to have left Vienna safely. Nobody had given anything away. When Rollo Martins left Dr Winkler's he was in no danger. He could have gone to bed at Sacher's and slept with a quiet mind. Unfortunately for him, he chose to go back to Harry's flat. He wanted to talk to the little man in the flat next to Harry's who said he had seen the accident – or had he really not said so much?

Perhaps the little man – who bore the name of Koch – had drunk a glass too much, perhaps he had simply spent a good day at the office, but this time, when Rollo Martins rang his bell, he was friendly and quite ready to talk. "Ah, I remember you. You are Herr Lime's friend."

He led the way into the sitting-room. "Ah, in the old days I would have offered you a cup of coffee. But now . . ."

Martins offered him a cigarette. He said, "Did you tell me that you had seen the accident?"

Koch looked at his wife. "The inquest is over. There is no harm. The gentleman is a friend. Yes, I saw the accident, but you are the only one who knows. When I say that I saw it, perhaps I should say that I heard it. But I got to the window in time to see them carry the body to the house."

"Was he in great pain?"

"He was dead."

"But the others say that he did not die at once."

"Perhaps they do not know death as well as I do."

"He was dead, of course, when the doctor arrived. He told me that."

"He was dead at once. You can take my word for it."

"I think, Herr Koch, that you should have gone to the inquest and told them what you saw."

"One must look after oneself, Herr Martins. I was not the only one who should have been there."

"What do you mean?"

"There were three people who helped to carry your friend to the house."

"I know – two men and the driver."

"The driver stayed where he was. He was very much shaken, poor man."

"Three men ... Can you describe them?"

But Herr Koch could not describe them. He had noticed only the man with the toupée. He had seen them from above. They had not looked up, and he had quickly looked away and closed the window. Martins no longer doubted that murder had been done. Why else had they lied about the moment of death? And the third man? Who was he?

He said, "Did you see Herr Lime go out?"

"No."

A new thought came to Martins: there was nothing – except the word of Kurtz and Cooler and the driver – to prove that in fact Harry had been killed at that moment.

"Herr Martin, I was just thinking – you are staying in Vienna?"

"Yes."

"If you want a place to live, you might get Herr Lime's flat."

"Who has the keys?"

"I have them."

"Could I see the flat?"

Herr Koch led the way into the flat that had been Harry's. In the little dark hall there was still the smell of cigarette smoke – the Turkish cigarettes that Harry always smoked. In the sitting-room the chairs had been pushed up against the walls. In the bedroom the bed was fresh and clean. "You see," Herr Koch said, "it is quite ready for a newcomer. My wife has cleaned up."

"Were there no papers, Herr Koch?"

"Herr Lime never left things lying around. His *brief-case* was full, but his friend took that away."

briefcase

"His friend?"

"Yes, the gentleman with the toupée."

It was possible, of course, that Lime had almost been expecting to die. Perhaps he had hoped that Martins would arrive in time to help. He said to Herr Koch, "I believe my friend was murdered."

"Murdered?" Herr Koch's friendliness disappeared. "I asked you in, and now you start talking nonsense."

"Why should it be nonsense?"

"We do not have murders in this zone. And you must leave here at once, please." He took Martins quickly out through the hall. Before he loudly shut his own door, Herr Koch's last word was, "It's no concern of mine." Poor Herr Koch! We do not choose our concerns.

Later, when I was questioning Martins, I said to him, "Did you see anybody at all on the stairs, or in the street outside?"

"Nobody." And I believed him. He said, "I noticed myself how quiet and dead the whole street looked. I could hear my own feet in the snow."

"Of course it proves nothing," I said. "Somebody could have followed you and hidden in a doorway."

"Yes."

"Or your whole story may be false."

"Yes."

"You came out here to join Lime, perhaps to help him . . ."

Martins said to me, "What was this racket you keep talking about?"

"I would have told you when I first saw you, but you got too angry. Now, I don't think it is wise to tell you. I don't like the people you meet, and besides our information is not complete."

"I'll believe that all right. I could think up a better detective than you in my bath."

On returning to Sacher's after his interview with Herr Koch, Martins found a note from Crabbin. "I have been trying to find you all day," Crabbin wrote. "We must meet and work out a programme for you. I have arranged for you to go to Innsbruck and Salzburg to give *lectures*. I would suggest a lecture on religion, and another called 'The Novel in England today.' Many people here would like to meet you, and I want to

lecture, a formal talk on a prepared subject

arrange a party for early next week. But I must have a word with you. You will be at the meeting tomorrow night, won't you? We all expect you at 8.30, and look forward to your coming. I will send transport to the hotel at 8.15 sharp."

Rollo Martins read the letter and went to bed.

8

It was nearly five o'clock when Rollo Martins reached Cooler's flat, which was over an ice-cream bar in the American zone. The bar was full of *G.I.*s with their girls, and the noise of long spoons and laughter followed him up the stairs. Again the card marked "Harry's friend" opened the doors for him. Cooler was in officer's uniform. His handshake was the most friendly act that Martins had met in Vienna.

"Any friend of Harry is all right with me," Cooler said. "I've heard of you, of course."

"From Harry?"

"I'm a great reader of Westerns," Cooler said, and Martins believed him as he had not believed Kurtz.

"I wondered – you were there, weren't you? – if you would tell me about Harry's death."

"It was a terrible thing," Cooler said. "I was just crossing the road to go to Harry. He and Kurtz were on the other side. Maybe if I hadn't started across the road, he would have stayed where he was. But he saw me and stepped off to meet me, and this jeep – it was terrible. Have a whisky, Mr Martins. It's silly of me, but I get shaken up when I think of it." He said as he put in the soda-water, "In spite of this uniform, I had never seen a man killed before."

"Was the other man in the car?"

Cooler took a long drink. "What man would you be speaking about, Mr Martins?"

"I was told there was another man there."

G.I., (Government Issue), American soldier

"I don't know how you got that idea." He poured out two more drinks. "There were just the three of us – me and Mr Kurtz and the driver. The doctor, of course. I expect you were thinking of the doctor."

"This man I was talking to happened to look out of the window – he has the flat next to Harry's. He said he saw three men and the driver. That's before the doctor arrived."

"He didn't say that at the inquest. It was his duty." Cooler looked at his glass. "It is strange, Mr Martins, with accidents. You'll never get two people who agree on what they have seen. Even Kurtz and I did not agree on details. Things happen so quickly, and then you have to try to remember them afterwards. Your man probably couldn't remember what happened before and what after. So he couldn't see the difference between the four of us."

"The four?"

"I was counting Harry. What else did he see, Mr Martins?"

"Nothing of interest – except he says Harry was dead when he was carried to the house."

"Well, he was dying – not much difference. Have another drink, Mr Martins?"

"No, I don't think I will."

"Well, I'd like one. I was very fond of your friend, Mr Martins, and I don't like talking about it."

"Perhaps one more drink – to keep you company. Do you know Anna Schmidt?"

"Harry's girl? I met her once, that's all. I helped Harry fix her papers. Not a thing one should say to strangers."

"What was wrong?"

"She was Hungarian and her father had been a Nazi, so they said."

"You took her some money from Harry, didn't you?"

The telephone rang, and Cooler emptied his glass. "Hullo" he said. "Why, yes. This is Colonel Cooler."

Then he sat with the receiver at his ear, listening to a voice a long way off. "Yes," he said once. He looked at Martins and seemed to look through him. He said, "You did quite right," and then, "Of course they will be sent. I gave you my word. Goodbye."

He put the receiver down. It was as if he was trying to remember something he had to do. Martins said, "Had you heard anything of this racket the police talk about?"

"I'm sorry. What's that?"

"They say Harry was in some racket."

"Oh, no," Cooler said. "No. That's quite impossible. He had a great sense of duty."

"Kurtz seemed to think it was possible."

"Kurtz does not understand how an Englishman feels," Cooler answered.

9

It was nearly dark when Martins made his way along the banks of the canal. Coming up the Kärntnerstrasse, he passed the door of the Military Police station. The four men of the International *Patrol* were climbing into their jeep; the Russian military policeman sat beside the driver (for the Russians were in charge for the next four weeks), and the Englishman, the American, and the Frenchman climbed up behind. Martins moved on, towards the only girl he knew in Vienna.

I asked him how he knew where she lived. Oh, he said, he had looked up her address on a map. He was good with maps, and knew how to find his way about.

Luckily she was in, sitting alone in her cold room. He said, "I thought I would just come in and see you. I was just passing..."

"Passing? Where to?"

"I had too much whisky with Colonel Cooler. I took a walk and came this way."

"I can't give you a drink here. Except tea. There's some of that packet left."

"No, thank you." He said, "Can I stay a little?"

"I wish you would." He sat down on the bed, and he told me a long time later that there it was he took his second real look at her.

"One of those bad days?" he asked.

"It's always bad about this time." She explained, "He used to come in, and when I heard you ring, just

---

patrol, group of police who drive round the city to see that all is well

for a moment I thought . . ." She sat down on a hard chair opposite Martins and said, "Please talk. You knew him. Just tell me anything."

And so he talked. The sky grew black outside the window while he talked. He noticed after a while that their hands had met. He said to me, "I never meant to fall in love, not with Harry's girl."

"When did it happen?" I asked him.

"It was very cold, and I got up to close the window *curtains*. I only noticed my hand was on hers when I took it away. As I stood up I looked down at her face and she was looking up. It wasn't a beautiful face – that was the trouble. It was a face to live with, day by day. I had always thought it was beauty one loved in a woman. I stood there at the curtains, waiting to close them, looking out. I couldn't see anything but my own face, looking back into the room, looking for her. She said, 'And what did Harry do that time?' and I wanted to say, 'Don't let us talk about Harry. He's dead. The dead are made to be forgotten.' Instead, of course, all I said was, 'What do you think? He just whistled his old tune as if nothing was the matter.' And I whistled the tune to her as well as I could. I heard her take a sudden breath, and I looked round. Without thinking, I said, 'He's dead. You can't go on remembering him for ever.'"

She said, "I know, but perhaps something will happen first."

"What do you mean - something happen?"

"Oh, I mean perhaps there will be another war, or I'll die, or the Russians will take me."

"You'll forget him in time. You'll fall in love again."

"I know, but I don't want to. Don't you see I don't want to?"

So Rollo Martins came back from the window and sat down on the bed again. When he had risen half a minute before, he had been the friend of Harry, trying to help Harry's girl. Now he was a man in love with Anna Schmidt. And Anna Schmidt had been in love with a man they had both known called Harry Lime. Martins didn't speak that evening about the past. Instead, he began to tell her of the people he had seen. "I can believe anything of Winkler," he told her. "But Cooler - I liked Cooler. He was the only one of his friends who stood up for Harry. The trouble is, if Cooler is right, then Koch is wrong. And I really thought I had something there."

"Who's Koch?"

Martins explained how he had returned to Harry's flat. He described his interview with Koch, and the story of the third man.

"If it's true," she said, "it's very important. And it means that they lied, Kurtz and Cooler."

"They might have lied to keep a friend out of trouble – if he was a friend."

"Yet another friend – on the spot. And how can Cooler be telling the truth then?"

"What do we do? Koch turned me out of his flat."

"He won't turn me out," she said, "or his wife won't. Let's go and see them."

They walked up the long road to Koch's flat together; the snow stuck to their shoes and made them move slowly. Anna Schmidt said, "Is it far?"

"Not very far now. Do you see that group of people up the road? It's somewhere about there." The group stood out in black against the whiteness. When they came a little nearer Martins said, "I think that's his building. What do you suppose this is, a political demonstration?"

Anna Schmidt stopped. She said, "Who else have you told about Koch?"

"Only you and Cooler. Why?"

"I'm frightened. It reminds me . . ." She was looking at the crowd. "Let's go away," she begged him.

"Don't be silly. We're on to something here, something big . . ."

"I'll wait for you."

"But you're going to talk to Koch."

"Find out first what all those people . . ."

He walked slowly on alone. The crowd was outside

the house where Koch lived. A man looked hard at him and said, "Are you another of them?"

"What do you mean?"

"The police."

"No. What are they doing?"

"They've been in and out all day."

"What's everybody waiting for?"

"They want to see him brought out."

"Who?"

"Herr Koch."

"What's he done?"

"Nobody knows that yet. They can't make up their minds in there – he might have killed himself, or it might be murder."

"Herr Koch?"

"Of course."

People were speaking of a foreigner who had visited Koch. A child, standing with his father, pointed at Martins and said, "He's a foreigner too." The father laughed.

Then the child called, "They are coming out."

A group of policemen carried a *stretcher* out. Frau Koch followed. Someone gave her a hand, and she looked round at this crowd of strangers.

Walking back down the street towards Anna, Martins looked back once. He said to Anna, "Koch has been murdered. Come away from here." He walked as fast as the snow would let him. The words of the child seemed to spread like a cloud over the city. Martins did not listen when Anna said to him, "Then what Koch said was true. There **was** a third man." Nor did he listen a little later when she said, "It must have been murder. You don't kill a man to hide anything less."

Martins said, "You had better go home alone. I'll keep away from you a little while till things are clearer."

Before she left him, she said, "Be careful. Koch knew so very little and they murdered him. You know as much as Koch."

At Sacher's the porter said, "Colonel Calloway has been in, asking for you, sir. He's in the bar."

"Back in a moment," Martins said and walked straight out of the hotel again: he wanted time to think. But immediately he stepped outside, a man came forward and said politely but firmly, "Please, sir." The man threw open the door of a khaki-painted car with a *Union Jack* on the front, and firmly asked Martins to get in. He got in without argument; sooner or later, he felt sure, the police would be asking questions.

The driver drove too fast on the frozen road, and Martins asked him not to. The only reply was something about "orders" – the rest he could not hear. "Have you orders to kill me?" Martins asked as a joke, and got no reply at all.

At least, Martins thought, I am not under arrest: they have not sent a guard; I am being asked to go to the police station and make a statement.

The car stopped, and the driver led the way up the stairs; he rang the bell of a great double door, and Martins heard many voices behind it. He turned sharply to the driver and said angrily, "Where are we, then?" But the driver was already half-way down the stairs, and already the door was opening. There stood Crabbin. "Oh, Mr Dexter, we have been so worried, but better late than never. Now please come and meet these people."

Martins said to Mr Crabbin, "I'm sorry, but –"

"Don't think any more about it," Mr Crabbin said. "One cup of coffee and then let's go on to the discussion. We have a very good crowd tonight." A young man placed a cup in his hand, and another put sugar in without asking. A third young man said into his ear, "Would you mind signing one of your books, Mr Dexter?" A large woman in black came up to him and said, "I don't mind if others hear me, but I don't like your books. I think a novel should tell a good story."

"So do I," Martins said hopelessly.

Union Jack, the British flag

An old lady said, "I do not read many English books, Mr Dexter, but I am told that yours . . ."

"Please finish your coffee," Crabbin said, and led him into an inner room. A number of *elderly* people were sitting on chairs in a half circle, waiting.

Martins was not able to tell me very much about the meeting; he was still thinking of Koch's death. The room was full of serious people interested in serious English literature, asking Martins questions that he could not answer. A woman in a brown hat said, "May I ask Mr Dexter if he is writing another book?"

"Oh yes – yes."

"May I ask the title?"

"'The Third Man'," Martins said, and felt better.

"Mr Dexter, could you tell us what writer has influenced you most?"

Martins, without thinking, said, "Grey." He meant, of course, the author of Riders of the Purple Sage, and he was pleased to find that people liked his answer. But an elderly lady asked, "Grey. What Grey? I do not know that name."

Martins said, "*Zane Grey* – I don't know any other," and did not quite understand the laughter that came from the English people present.

"This is a little joke of Mr Dexter's," said Crabbin. "He meant the poet *Gray*."

---

elderly, old but not very old
Zane Grey (1872–1939), American writer, known for his novels about cowboys in the U.S. West, particularly Riders of the Purple Sage (1912)
Thomas Gray (1716–1771), English poet, whose Elegy Written in a Country Churchyard (1751) is one of the best known of English lyric poems

"And he is called Zane Grey?"

"That was Mr Dexter's joke. Zane Grey wrote what we call Westerns – cheap short novels about cowboys."

"He is not a great writer?"

"No, no. Far from it," Mr Crabbin said.

Martins found the rest of the evening very difficult. He remembered very little more before Crabbin was making a speech to thank him. Then one of the young men led him to a table loaded with books and asked him to sign them. The books were by the English novelist Benjamin Dexter. "What have I got to do?"

"Just put your name in the books. That's all they expect. But I would be so happy if you would just write something more in my copy."

Martins took his pen and wrote: "From B. Dexter, author of The Lone Rider of Santa Fé," and the young man read it, took the book and went to show it to Crabbin, who smiled and moved his head up and down, up and down. "B. Dexter, B. Dexter, B. Dexter," Martins wrote quickly – it was not, after all, a lie. Every time he took another book and looked up, he met Crabbin's eye. People were beginning to leave, when suddenly in the mirror Martins saw a military policeman. This man seemed to be having a discussion with one of Crabbin's young men. There was only one book left to sign. Martins wrote "B. Dexter" and started for the door.

"And this gentleman?" the policeman asked.

"It's Mr Benjamin Dexter," the young man said.

"Toilet. Is there a toilet?" Martins asked.

"I understand a Mr Rollo Martins came here in one of your cars."

"A mistake, clearly a mistake."

"Second door on the left," the young man said.

Martins took his coat and started down the stairs. On the first floor he heard someone coming up. Looking over, he saw Paine, whom I had sent to find him. Martins opened a door and shut it behind him. He heard Paine go by. The room where Martins stood was dark, but a sound made him turn.

He could see nothing, and the sound died away. Outside, somebody called, "Mr Dexter, Mr Dexter." Then a new sound started in the dark room. It was like somebody whispering. Martins said, "Is anybody there?" and the sound stopped again. It was too much for him. He took out his *lighter.* Footsteps went by and down the stairs. He tried the lighter again and again and no light came. Somebody moved in the dark. He

---

lighter, see picture, page 56

asked once more with the anger of fear, "Is anybody there?" He felt for a *switch*, first to his right hand and then to his left. Then he was afraid that he had lost the door, and felt for the *knob.* He was far less afraid of the police than of the darkness, and he had no idea of the noise he was making.

Paine heard the noise from the bottom of the stairs and came back. He switched on the light by the stairs, and Martins saw the light under the door. He opened the door and, smiling weakly at Paine, turned back to take a look at the room. The eyes of a *parrot* stared back at him. "We were looking for you, sir," said Paine. "Colonel Calloway wants a word with you."

"I lost my way," Martins said.

"Yes, sir. We thought that was what had happened."

10

I had carefully noted all Martins' movements. He had been seen with Kurtz, and at the Josefstadt Theatre. I knew about his visit to Dr Winkler and to Colonel Cooler, and his first return to the house where Harry had lived. For some reason my man lost him between Cooler's and Anna Schmidt's flats; the man reported that Martins had walked around a lot. I tried to pick Martins up at the hotel and just missed him. It seemed to me that the time had come for another interview, this time at my office.

I put a good wide desk between us and gave him a cigarette. I asked him about Kurtz, and he told me what I knew already. I then asked him about Anna Schmidt. I understood from his reply that he must have been with her after visiting Colonel Cooler; that filled in one of the missing points. "You've been getting around," I said, "quite a bit. And have you found out anything about your friend?"

"Oh, yes," he said. "It was under your nose but you didn't see it."

"What?"

"That he was murdered." That took me by surprise. I had at one time thought that Lime might have killed himself, but I had given up that idea.

"Go on," I said. Martins tried not to mention Koch, just talking about somebody who had seen the accident. So I didn't at first understand why the third man should be so important.

"He didn't come to the inquest, and the others lied to keep him out."

"It was an accident, and why get another man in trouble?"

"There was more to it than that. The little man who told me about it – they've murdered him. They killed him because they didn't know what else he might have seen."

"Now we have it," I said. "You mean Koch."

"Yes."

"As far as we know, you were the last person to see Koch alive. The Austrian police think you might have killed him. Who else knew about your visit to Koch?"

"I told Cooler." Martins said, "Suppose after I left he telephoned the story to someone – to the third man. They had to stop Koch's mouth."

"Koch was killed soon after nine. You returned to Sacher's at nine-thirty. Where were you before that?"

"Walking around and thinking things over."

"You can't prove that this is true?"

"No."

I wanted to frighten Martins, so it was no use telling him that my men had followed him all the time. I knew that he hadn't killed Koch, but I was still unsure about him. The man who owns the knife is not always the real murderer.

"Can I have a cigarette?"

"Yes."

Martins said, "How did you know I went to Koch's? That was why you wanted me here, wasn't it?"

"The Austrian police –"

"They didn't know that I was the man who had visited Koch."

"Colonel Cooler telephoned me."

"Then that lets him out. If he had been in it, he

wouldn't have wanted you to know Koch's story."

"To tell you the truth, Cooler irritates me. Of course, he doesn't know that I know about his racket."

"Is he in a racket too?"

"Not a very serious one. He may have made twenty-five thousand dollars selling *tyres*. But let the Americans look after their own people."

"Is that the kind of thing Harry was doing?"

"No. It was more serious."

Martins said, "You know, Koch's death has shaken me. Perhaps Harry did get into something bad. Perhaps he was trying to get out again, and that was why they murdered him."

"Or perhaps," I said, "they wanted a bigger share of the money."

He did not get angry this time. He said, "I'm sorry about the other day."

"That's all right," I said. "I'll show you enough of the facts in Lime's case for you to understand. But I tell you, it's going to be a shock."

It couldn't help being a shock. The war and the peace let loose a great number of rackets, but none worse than the *penicillin* racket. Penicillin in Austria was only given to military hospitals. No *civilian* hospital could get it. At

tyre

---

penicillin, medicine to kill bacteria
civilian, not military

first, the penicillin racket was not too bad: the stuff was stolen in military hospitals and sold to Austrian doctors at very high prices. But then the racket began to get organized: the big men saw big money in it. They began adding water to the penicillin. Martins did not see the point. He said, "I suppose that makes the stuff useless."

I said, "We wouldn't worry so much if that was all, but just think. If the penicillin is too weak the first time, it won't work at all the second time. That's what often happens. Men have lost their arms and legs this way – and their lives. But perhaps what shocked me most was visiting the children's hospital here. The hospital had bought some of this stuff for use against *meningitis*. Some of the children simply died, and some of them went mad. You can see them now in a special hospital."

"You haven't proved yet that Harry –"

"We are coming to that now," I said. "Just sit still and listen. We put one of our men to work in the British Military Hospital, and finally he found the man who stole the penicillin – a man called Harbin. But even this led us only as far as Kurtz."

"Kurtz!" said Martins in surprise. "But why haven't you arrested him?"

"We are going to," I said.

Kurtz was a big step forward, for with Kurtz Lime sometimes put things on paper. "Look at this," I said, showing Martins a short note to Harbin written by Lime, and another note from Harbin to Kurtz.

At first Martins did not understand. But then he read the two notes carefully again.

---

meningitis, serious illness, caused by bacteria which attack the coverings of the brain

"You see what I mean?" I said.

He didn't say a word. Who would, when he sees a world laid in ruins before him? And this was the ruin of all his happy memories of Harry Lime – the dreams, the walks, the afternoons when they secretly shot rabbits, a world of easy friendship. While he sat there looking at his hands and saying nothing, I took out a bottle of whisky and poured out two large drinks. "Drink that," I said, and he did.

"Are you certain that he was the real boss?"

"We've not found anyone behind him so far."

"Suppose someone had forced him into it, as you forced Harbin."

"It's possible."

"And they murdered him in case he talked when he was arrested."

"It's not impossible."

"I'm glad they did," he said. "And in that case I might as well be getting back to England."

"I'd rather you didn't just now. The Austrian police might want a word with you."

"I see," he said.

"When we've found the third man . . ." I said.

"I'd like to hear him talk," he said. "The bastard. The bloody bastard."

11

After he left me, Martins went straight off to get *drunk*. He went from one night club to another and had drink after drink. In one place, the heating had failed and people sat in overcoats drinking cocktails. Then he went to see Anna. It must have been about three in the morning. He was now nearly *sober*. He had only one idea in his head, that Anna must be told about Harry too.

He said, "Anna, I've found out everything."

"Come in," she said. "You don't want to wake the whole house." The bed looked as if she had not slept.

"Now," she said, "what is it? I thought you were going to keep away. Are the police after you?"

"No."

"You didn't really kill Koch, did you?"

"Of course not."

"You're drunk aren't you?"

"I am a bit," he said. "I'm sorry."

"Why? I would like a drink myself."

He said, "I've been with the British police. They know I didn't do it. But I've learnt everything from them. Harry was in a racket – a bad racket. He was no good at all. We were both wrong."

"You'd better tell me," Anna said. She sat down on the bed and he told her, bit by bit, about the penicillin and the dead children and the children who had gone mad. He stopped and they were silent.

---

drunk, drunken, full of alcoholic drink
sober, not drunk

She said, "Is that all?"

"Yes."

"You were sober when they told you? They really proved it?"

"Yes. So that, you see, was Harry."

"I'm glad he is dead now," she said. "I wouldn't have wanted him to be in prison."

"But can you understand how Harry – your Harry, my Harry – could have got into a racket like that? I feel as though he had never really existed, that we had dreamed him. Was he laughing at fools like us all the time?"

"He may have been. What does it matter?" she said. "Sit down. Don't worry. If he was alive now, he might be able to explain, but we've got to remember him as he was to us."

"Those children –"

She said angrily, "Harry was real. He wasn't just your hero and my lover. He was Harry. He was in a racket. He did bad things. What about it? He was the man we knew."

He said, "Stop trying to be so wise! Don't you see that I love you?"

She looked at him in great surprise. "You?"

"Yes, me."

She said, "But I don't even know what colour your eyes are."

"Can't you get him out of your mind?"

"No."

He said, "As soon as they have cleared up this Koch murder, I'm leaving Vienna. I can't feel interested any longer in whether Kurtz killed Harry – or the third man. But you still love him. You love a cheat, a murderer."

"I loved a man," she said. "I told you – a man is still a man even if you find out more about him."

"I hate the way you talk."

"I didn't ask you to come."

"You make me angry."

She laughed. "You are so comic. You come here at three in the morning – a stranger – and say you love me. Then you get angry. What do you expect me to do – or say?"

"I haven't seen you laugh before. Do it again. I like it."

"Come away from the window. There are no curtains."

"There's nobody to see us." But he wasn't quite sure: down in the street, a long shadow that had moved stood still again. He said, "You still love Harry, don't you?"

"Yes."

"Perhaps I do. I don't know." He stood away from her and said, "I'll be going."

He walked quickly away. He didn't turn round to see whether he was being followed. But, passing by the end of a street, he turned and saw, just around the corner, pressed against a wall, a thick figure. Martins stopped and stared. It looked like somebody he knew. Perhaps it was it was one of those who had followed him to see where he was going. Martins stood there, staring at the silent figure who stared back at him. A policeman, perhaps, or one of those men who had forced Harry into the racket and then killed him - or even possibly the third man?

He called sharply, "Do you want anything?" and there was no reply. He called again, "Answer, can't you?" And an answer came, for a window curtain was drawn back by some sleeper he had awakened, and the light fell across the street and lit up the face of Harry Lime.

the
advertisement
kiosk

12

"Do you believe in *ghosts*?" Martins said to me.

"Do you?"

"I do now."

"I also believe that drunken men see things - sometimes *rats*, sometimes worse."

He hadn't come to me at once with his story - only the danger to Anna Schmidt drove him back into my office. He said, "If it had been just the face, I wouldn't have worried. I had been thinking of Harry, and I might easily have mistaken a stranger. The light was turned off again at once, you see, and the man ran away down the street - if he was a man. I was so surprised that I stood still for five seconds or more while the man ran. He came to one of those *advertisement kiosks*, and for a moment he moved out of sight. I ran after him. It only took me ten seconds to reach the kiosk, but the strange thing was that he never appeared again. I reached the kiosk. There wasn't anybody there, and the street was empty."

rat

ghost

"What did you do then?"

"I had to have another drink. My nerves were all in pieces."

"Didn't that bring him back?"

"No, but it sent me back to Anna's."

I think he only came to me with this absurd story because of what happened to Anna. My theory, when he did tell me the story, was that somebody had watched him, and that this somebody had warned a member of the penicillin *ring* by telephone. Things happened fast that night.

Rollo Martins went drunkenly back at four o'clock, intending to tell Anna that he had seen the ghost of Harry. Outside Anna's flat, he met a frightened porter who told him that she had been taken away by the International Patrol.

What happened was this. Half-way through the patrol, the Russian policemen directed the car to the street where Anna lived. The British policeman that night was new to the job: he didn't realize, till the other two told him, that they had entered the British zone. He spoke a little German and no French, and the Frenchman gave up trying to explain to him. The American took on the job. "It's all right by me," he said, "but is it all right by you?" The British policeman touched the Russian's shoulder. The latter turned his Mongol face and sent a stream of language at him which he could not understand. Outside the building where Anna lived, the American asked in German what it was all about. The Russian dug out a few words of German and waved some papers. As far as they could understand, some

---

ring, the group of people working in the racket

Russian woman wanted by the Russian police was living there without papers. They went upstairs and the Russian tried Anna's door. It was locked, but he put his shoulder to it and it flew open. Anna was in bed, though I don't suppose she was asleep.

There is a lot of comedy in these situations if you are not in them. The Russian, you see, refused to leave the room while Anna dressed; the Englishman refused to remain in the room; the American wouldn't leave a girl alone with a Russian soldier, so he turned his back; and the Frenchman – well, I think the Frenchman must have thought it was fun, for he was watching Anna in the mirror.

I don't want you to think that the Englishman came too badly out of the affair. Outside the door, he had time to think, and his thoughts led him to the telephone in the next flat. He got straight through to me at my flat and woke me out of that deepest middle sleep. That was why, when Martins rang me up an hour later, I already knew what was worrying him. He never said anything bad about policemen after that night.

If the International Patrol made an arrest, they had to take the prisoner to the International Headquarters. This was what the Russian was trying not to do. But I had given my orders to the British policeman.

When he went back to Anna's room there was a quarrel. Anna had told the American that she had Austrian papers (which was true) and that they were quite in order (which was not quite true). The American told the Russian in bad German that they had no right to arrest an Austrian. The American asked Anna for her papers and when she tried to hand them over, the Russian took them from her hand.

"Hungarian," he said, "Hungarian - bad, bad."

The American, whose name was O'Brien, said, "Give the girl back her papers," which the Russian did not understand. The American put his hand on his gun, and the British policeman said gently to him, "Let it go."

"If those papers are not in order, we have got a right to look," said the American.

"Just let it go. We'll see them at *HQ*."

"If we get to HQ. You can't trust these Russian drivers. Probably he'll drive right through to the Russian zone."

"We'll see," said the British policeman.

They got back into the car with Anna, who sat in front between the two Russians, so afraid she could not say a word. After they had gone a little way, the American touched the Russian on the shoulder. "Wrong way," he said. "HQ that way."

The Russian spoke away in his own language while they drove on. "It's what I said," O'Brien told the Englishman. "They are taking her to the Russian zone." Anna stared out in panic. "Don't worry, little girl," O'Brien said. "I'll fix them all right."

The driver stopped suddenly: the road was blocked. You see, I knew they would have to pass this military post if they did not drive to the International HQ. I put my head in at the car window and said to the Russian, "What are you doing in the British zone?"

He said it was "orders".

"Whose orders? Let me see them." I noted the name signed at the bottom. I said, "This tells you to pick up a certain Hungarian woman who is living with false papers in the British zone. Let me see the papers."

He started on a long explanation, but I saw the papers in his pocket, and I pulled them out. He put his

---

HQ, headquarters

hand on his gun, and I hit him in the face. That made him quiet – that and seeing three British soldiers coming up to the car. I said, "These papers look to me quite in order, but I'll examine them and send a report to your colonel. He can, of course, have the lady sent over at any time." I said to Anna, "Get out of the car." She couldn't get by the Russian, so I had to pull him out first. Then I put a packet of cigarettes in his hand, said, "Have a good smoke," waved my hand to the others, and that was the end of that.

13

While Martins told me how he went back to Anna's and found her gone, I did some hard thinking. I wasn't satisfied with the ghost story, or the idea that the face of Harry Lime had only been imagined by the drunken Martins. I rang up my assistant and asked him if he knew where Harbin was. He said no. "All right," I said. "Go on trying to get hold of him."

"You know, sir, we should have thought that it might be murder. There are one or two points –"

"Put them on paper, Carter."

"Yes, sir. I think, sir, if you don't mind my saying so, we ought to have the body dug up. He may not have died just when the others said."

"I agree, Carter."

Martins was right. I had made a fool of myself.

I turned to Martins again and said, "Did you look inside the kiosk or was it locked?"

"Oh, it was just one of those solid iron kiosks you see everywhere."

"You had better show me the place."

"But is Anna all right?"

"The police are watching her flat."

I didn't want to frighten people with a police car, so we went into the district on foot. Martins led me down a side street. We stopped at the kiosk. "You see, he passed behind here, and simply disappeared – into the ground."

"That is exactly where he did go," I said.

"How do you mean?"

Martins had clearly not noticed that the kiosk had

a door. I pulled it open and showed him the little iron *staircase* that disappeared into the ground. He said, "Good God, then I didn't imagine him!"

"It's one of the entrances to the main *sewer.*"

"And anyone can go down?"

"Anyone. For some reason the Russians don't want these doors locked."

"How far can one go?"

"Right across Vienna. People used the sewers during the war; some people hid there for two years. The Austrians have special police for patrolling these sewers." I closed the door of the kiosk again. I said, "So that's how your friend disappeared."

"You really believe it was Harry?"

"Everything points that way."

"Then whom did they bury?"

"I don't know yet, but we soon shall, because we are digging the body up again. I've got an idea that Koch was not the only man they murdered."

Martins said, "It's a bit of a shock."

"Yes."

"What are you going to do about it?"

"I don't know."

Martins said, "I wish I could speak to him. You see, there's so much I simply can't believe."

"Perhaps you are the only one who could speak to him. There is a risk, though, because you know too much."

"I still can't believe it – I only saw the face for a moment." He said, "What shall I do?"

---

sewer, large underground passage for waste water. See picture, page 88

"He won't leave the Russian zone now. Perhaps that's why he tried to have the girl taken over – because he loves her? I don't know. I do know that the only person who could make him come over would be you – or her, if he still believes you are his friend. But first you've got to speak to him. I can't see how."

"I could go and see Kurtz. I have the address."

I said, "Remember. Lime may not want you to leave the Russian zone when once you are there, and I can't protect you there."

"I want to clear the whole thing up," Martins said. "I don't want to help you to catch him, but I'll talk to him. That's all."

14

Martins was careful to carry with him all his papers, including the one that allowed him to move freely through all the zones of Vienna. He walked through into the Russian zone, where he had no difficulty in finding Kurtz's flat. When he rang the bell, the door was opened by Kurtz himself.

"Oh," Kurtz said, "it's you, Mr Martins," and put his hand to the back of his head. Kurtz was not wearing his toupée. And he had a perfectly normal head of hair, close cut. Kurtz said, "It would have been better to have telephoned me. You nearly missed me. I was going out."

"May I come in a moment?"

"Of course."

In the hall Martins saw Kurtz's overcoat, his raincoat, a couple of hats and the toupée. He said, "I'm glad to see your hair has grown."

"It keeps the head warm," said Kurtz.

"Whose head?" said Martin, for he had suddenly thought how useful that toupée might have been on the day of the accident. "Never mind," he went on quickly. "I'm here to see Harry."

"Harry?"

"I want to talk to him."

"Are you mad?"

"I'm in a hurry, so let us suppose that I am. But if you see Harry – or his ghost – let him know that I want to talk to him. A ghost isn't afraid of a man, is it? Surely it's the other way round. I'll be waiting in the *Prater* by the *Big Wheel* for the next two hours –

In the Prater park

if you can get in touch with the dead." He added, "Remember I was Harry's friend."

Kurtz said nothing, but somewhere in another room, Martins heard someone sneeze. Martins threw open a door: he had half expected to see the dead rise again, but it was only Dr Winkler who rose from a kitchen chair.

Martins said to Kurtz, "Tell the doctor about my madness. He might be able to explain it. And remember the place – the Big Wheel. Or do ghosts only rise by night?" He left the flat.

For an hour he waited near the Big Wheel, walking up and down to keep warm. The Prater was nearly empty. A few children were playing, and a few young couples entered the *cars* of the Wheel. Martins wondered who would come for him. Was there enough friendship left in Harry for him to come alone, or would he bring the police with him? And then Martins wondered: Was it all just a drunken man's picture? Are they digging up Harry's body now in the Central Cemetery?

Somewhere a man was whistling, and Martins knew the tune. He turned and waited. His heart beat faster. Was it fear, or was it the quickness that Harry had always brought into life when he came? He came now, as though nothing much had happened.

"Harry."

"Hullo, Rollo."

Harry Lime didn't make the mistake of putting out a hand that Martins might not have taken. Instead, he just touched Martins' arm and said, "How are things?"

"We've got to talk, Harry."

---

car, see picture, page 77

"Of course."

"Alone."

"We couldn't be more alone than here."

Harry had always known how to do things, and even here he knew. He gave the woman in charge of the Wheel some extra money, so that they might have a car to themselves. He said, "Lovers used to do this in the old days, but they haven't the money now." He looked out of the window of the car while the city sank very slowly on one side of them.

"Well," Harry said, "it's good to see you, Rollo."

"I was at your funeral."

"That was pretty clever of me, wasn't it?"

"Not so clever for your girl. She was there too – in tears."

"She is a good little thing," Harry said. "I'm very fond of her."

"I didn't believe the police when they told me about you."

Harry said, "When I asked you to come, I didn't know what was going to happen. I didn't think the police had found out anything about me."

"Were you going to share the money with me?"

"I've never kept you out of anything, old man, yet." He stood with his back to the door as the car swung up, and smiled back at Rollo Martins. Martins remembered him as a schoolboy standing like that and saying, "I've learned a way to get out at night. It's absolutely safe. You are the only one I am telling about it." Martins thought: He has never grown up.

To Harry he said, "Have you ever visited the children's hospital? To see the results of your work?"

Harry felt the back of the door with his hand. "Look

down there, Rollo," he said. "Would you feel any pity if any of those little *dots* stopped moving – for ever? If I said you could have twenty thousand pounds for every dot that stops, would you really, old man, tell me to keep the money?"

"You are finished now. The police know everything."

"But they can't catch me, Rollo, you'll see. I'll come

---

dot, little black spot

up again. You can't keep a good man down."

The car stopped at the highest point. Harry turned his back and looked out of the window. Martins thought: One good push and I could break the glass, and he imagined the body falling, falling. He said, "You know the police are planning to dig up your body? What will they find?"

"Harbin," Harry replied simply. He turned away from the window and said, "Look at the sky."

The sun had gone down and the sky was red.

"Why did the Russians try to take Anna?"

"She had false papers, old man."

"Who told them?"

"There is a price for living in this zone, Rollo. I have to give them a little information now and then."

"She loves you."

"Well, I gave her a good time while it lasted."

"And I love her."

"That's fine, old man. Be kind to her. And you can help to keep her mouth shut."

"I'd like to knock you through the window."

"But you won't, old man. I would trust you anywhere, Rollo. Kurtz didn't want me to come, but I know you. Then he wanted me to arrange an accident. He told me it would be easy in this car."

"Except that I am the stronger of us."

"But I'm the one with the gun. You don't think they would be able to see what had happened when you hit the ground?" Again the car began to move. "What fools we are, Rollo, talking like this, as if I would do that to you - or you to me." He turned his back and leaned his face against the glass. "How much do your books give you a year?"

"A thousand."

"And you pay *tax*. I make thirty thousand, free."

"You used to be a Catholic."

"Oh, I still believe. In God and kindness and all that. I'm not hurting anybody's soul by what I do. The dead are happier dead. I could bring you in, you know. It would be useful. I have no one left in the Inner City."

"Except Cooler? And Winkler?"

"You mustn't turn into a policeman, old man." They left the car and he put his hand on Martins' arm. "Have you heard anything of our old friend Bracer?"

"I had a card at Christmas."

"Those were the days, old man. Well, I've got to leave you here. We'll see each other some time. If you are in trouble, you can always get me at Kurtz's." He moved away and, turning, waved his hand. It was like the whole past moving off under a cloud. Martins suddenly called after him, "Don't trust me, Harry," but there was too great a distance between them for the words to carry.

---

tax, part of the money a person earns that has to be paid to the State

15

"Anna was at the theatre," Martins told me. "She acted badly – she wasn't much of an actress at the best of times. I saw her afterwards in her dressing- room. I told her Harry was alive. I thought she would be glad, but she sat in front of her mirror and let the tears run down her face. I wished afterwards that she had been glad. She looked awful and I loved her. Then I told her about my interview with Harry, but she did not really listen. When I had finished she said, "I wish he was dead."

"He ought to be, after what he has done."

"I mean he would be safe then – from everybody."

I asked Martins, "Did you show her the photographs I gave you – of the children in the hospital?"

"Yes. I put them up in front of her and said, 'The police can't arrest Harry unless they get him into this zone, and we've got to help.'

"She said, 'I thought he was your friend.' I said, 'He **was** my friend.' She said, 'I'll never help you to get Harry. I don't want to see him again, I don't want to hear his voice, but I won't do a thing to hurt him.'"

I said to Martins, "And then?"

Martins said, "Oh, I just left her. Now it's your turn to work on me. What do you want me to do?"

"I want to act quickly. You see, it was Harbin's body in the coffin, so we can get Winkler and Cooler at once. Kurtz is out of our reach in the Russian zone, and so is the driver. A message should go from you to Lime at once. He must be made to believe that we brought you here for questioning as soon as you got back into the Inner City; that you heard from me about Harbin; and that you now see what has happened and go to warn Cooler. Cooler will go and see Kurtz, and Lime will know that you have played the game. Three hours later, you send a message to Lime that the police are after you and you must see him."

"He won't come."

"I'm not so sure. We'll find a place where we can hide – and where he thinks there is no risk. He would be pleased to know that he saved you from trouble, and it would stop your mouth."

Martins said, "He never used to save me from trouble at school."

"That wasn't such serious trouble."

Martins said, "I told Harry not to trust me, but he didn't hear."

"Do you agree?"

The photographs of the children were on my desk again. Martins took a long look at them. "Yes," he said, "I agree."

16

All the first part went according to plan. We did not arrest Winkler until after Cooler had been warned. Martins enjoyed his short interview with Cooler.

"Hullo, Mr Martins," said Cooler, "it's good to see you. Sit down. I am glad everything went off all right between you and Colonel Calloway."

"It didn't," Martins said.

"You mustn't be angry that I told him about you seeing Koch. I liked you, but I had to do my duty."

"Is it a duty to make false statements at an inquest?"

Cooler said, "Oh, that old story. I'm afraid you **are** angry with me –"

"The police have dug up the body. They'll be after you and Winkler. I want you to warn Harry . . ."

"I don't understand."

"Oh yes, you do." And it was clear that he did. Martins left him.

I studied a map of the sewer system. The entrance to the great sewer was placed, like all the others, in an advertisement kiosk. I decided that a café near that entrance would be the best place. There, Lime only had to come up, walk for twenty seconds, bring Martins back with him, and sink again into the darkness of the sewers. He probably knew that one patrol of the sewer police ended before midnight, and that the next did not start till two. So at midnight Martins sat in the little cold café near the kiosk, drinking coffee after coffee. I had lent him a revolver; I had men placed as close to the kiosk as I could, and the sewer police were ready. I intended, if I could, to catch Lime before he went underground again. It would save trouble – and save risk to Martins. So there in the café Martins sat.

There was no heating in the café, and Martins sat warming each hand in turn on cup after cup of watery coffee. There was one of my men with him most of the time, but I changed them every twenty minutes or so. More than an hour passed. Martins had long given up hope. So had I, where I waited at the phone several streets away, with a party of the sewer police. Suddenly the telephone rang. It was Martins. He said, "I'm dying with cold. It's a quarter past one. Is there any point in going on?"

"You shouldn't telephone. You must stay in sight."

Martins' voice said suddenly, "Christ, he's here. He's –" and then the telephone went dead. I said to my assistant, "Give the signal to guard all the sewer entrances," and to my sewer police, "We are going down." What had happened was this. Martins was still on the telephone when Harry Lime came into the café. I don't know what Lime heard, if he heard anything. Seeing a man speaking on the telephone would have been enough to warn him. Lime knew that that man was wanted by the police and was without friends in Vienna.

Lime was out of the café before Martins had put down the receiver. It was one of the few moments when none of my men was in the café. One man had just left, and another was outside waiting to go in. Harry Lime ran past him and towards the kiosk. Martins came out of the café and saw my men. If he had called out then, it would have been an easy shot. But I suppose it was not Lime, the penicillin racketeer, who was escaping down the street; it was Harry. Martins waited just long enough for Lime to put the kiosk between them. Then he called out, "That's him," but Lime was already underground.

What a strange world unknown to most of us lies under our feet. The main sewer, like a river half as wide as the Thames, rushes by under a huge *arch*, fed by smaller streams. These streams have fallen in waterfalls from higher levels and have been *purified* in their fall, so that the air is fresh and the darkness full of the sound of falling and rushing water. Martins and my policeman went down the staircase first, then walked along a side passage so low that they had to bend, and then they came to the river and the water flowed round their feet.

My man shone his *torch* along the edge of the water, showing up Lime's footprints. "He has gone that way. Keep behind me, sir, the bastard may shoot."

"Then why should you be in front?"

"It's my job, sir." The water came half-way up their legs as they walked. The policeman took out a whistle and blew, and very far away, here and again there, came the notes of a reply. He said, "The sewer police are all down here now. I wish my wife could see me now." He lifted his torch for a moment to shine it ahead, and at that moment the shot came. The torch flew out of his hand and fell in the water. He said, "The bloody bastard!"

"Are you hurt?"

"No, only my hand, that's all. A week off work.

---

arch, see picture, page 88
purify, make clean
torch, see picture, page 88

In the sewer

Here, sir, take this other torch, while I tie my hand up. Don't shine it. He is in one of the side passages." For a long time the sound of the shot went on echoing: when the last echo died away, a whistle blew ahead of them, and the policeman blew an answer.

Martins said, "It's a strange thing – I don't even know your name."

"Bates, sir."

Martins said, "Let me come in front. I don't think he'll shoot at me, and I want to talk to him."

"I had orders to look after you, sir. Be careful."

"That's all right."

He passed Bates and called out, "Harry," and the name sent up an echo, "Harry, Harry, Harry!"

A voice came out quite near. "Is that you, old man? What do you want me to do?"

"Come out. And put your hands above your head."

"I haven't a torch. I can't see a thing."

"Be careful, sir," said Bates.

"Stand against the wall. He won't shoot at me," Martins said. He called, "Harry, I'm going to shine the torch. Come out. You haven't got a chance."

He shone the torch, and twenty feet away Harry came out. "Hands above the head, Harry." Harry raised his hand and fired and Martins heard Bates cry out. At the same moment, a strong light lit the whole place. My party had reached the scene. Lime turned this way and that, blinded by the light like a rabbit in front of a car. Then suddenly he jumped into the rushing water, which carried him past the body of Bates into the dark. Martins had his gun in his hand. "There," I said. "There. Shoot." He lifted the gun and fired, just as he had fired at the same command all those years ago, at rabbits. And, as he did then, he failed to fire straight. A cry of pain rang out. "Well done," I called and stopped at Bates's body. He was dead, with his eyes open. I looked up and Martins was out of sight. Then I heard another shot.

Martins told me later, "I walked along to find Harry, but I must have missed him in the dark. I was afraid to lift the torch. I didn't want him to shoot again. When I fired, I must have hit him just at the entrance of a side passage. Then, I suppose, he crept painfully up the

passage to the foot of the iron stairs. Thirty feet above his head was the street. He began to pull himself up the stairs, but then the pain took him and he couldn't go on. Then – I don't know why – he whistled that tune, which I had been fool enough to believe he had written himself. I followed the sound and went carefully up the side passage towards him. 'Harry,' I said, and the whistling stopped, just above my head. I put my hand on the iron staircase and began to go up. Then, only three steps up, my foot touched his hand, and he was there. I shone my torch on him; he hadn't got a gun. For a moment I thought he was dead, but then he gave a little cry of pain. I said, 'Harry,' and he slowly turned his eyes to my face. He was trying to speak, and I bent down to listen. 'Bloody fool,' he said. I don't know if he meant that for himself or for me, with my thousand a year taxed and my imagined cowboys who couldn't even shoot a rabbit cleanly. Then he gave another little cry of pain. I couldn't bear it any more and I lifted my gun and fired."

"We'll forget that bit," I said.

Martins said, "I never shall."

17

The weather had turned warmer, and all over Vienna the snow melted. Electric drills were no longer needed to break the frozen ground. It was almost as warm as a spring day when Harry Lime had his second funeral. I was glad to get him under earth again, but it had taken two men's deaths. The group by the grave was smaller now: Kurtz wasn't there, nor Winkler – only the girl and Rollo Martins and myself.

After it was over, the girl walked away without a word to either of us. I said to Martins, "Today I've got transport. Can I take you into town?"

"No," he said, "I'll take a bus."

"You win. You've proved me a bloody fool."

"I haven't won," he said. "I've lost." I watched him walking after the girl. He caught her up and they walked side by side. I don't think he said a word to her. It was like the end of a story, except that very soon her hand was through his arm – which is how a story usually begins. He couldn't shoot straight, but he had a way with Westerns – and with girls. And Crabbin? Oh, Crabbin is still trying to make somebody pay Dexter's expenses. They say they can't pay at the same time in Stockholm and Vienna. Poor Crabbin. Poor all of us, when you come to think of it.

Questions (1)

1. What sort of person is telling the story?
2. Whose funeral is it?
3. Talk about Rollo Martins.

Questions (2)

1. How much do you think five pounds was worth?
2. Why has Martins come to Vienna?
3. What kind of books does Martins write, and under what name?
4. Do you know any good Westerns? Talk about them.
5. How did Lime die, according to the small man in the other flat? Give the exact words.
6. Was Rollo Martins good at shooting when he was at school? Explain.
7. Is the teller of the story (the narrator) sad that Lime is dead?
8. Why does the narrator follow Martins?
9. What is the name of the narrator?
10. What do you think: did Martins like Harry Lime?
11. What do you think Harry Lime's racket might have been?

12. Do you know the tune that Harry Lime whistled?
13. What part do you think the waiter plays?
14. What two things does Martins want to do to Calloway? Can you say why?
15. What parts of this chapter do you think would be good material for a film?

Questions (3)

1. Where does Paine take Martins?
2. How does Martins explain about his mouth?
3. Say what you know about Buck Dexter and Benjamin Dexter.
4. Who did Lime sometimes fetch at the Institute?
5. Who telephones Martins?
6. What does the stranger say about Harry's death?
7. Where and when is Martins to meet Kurtz?
8. How is Martins to know Kurtz?
9. What does Martins wonder about?

Questions (4)

1. How did Lime die, according to Kurtz? Give the exact words.
2. Did Lime die immediately?

3. What is an inquest?
4. Whose addresses does Martins want?
5. Is Martins satisfied with the stories of Harry's death?
6. What language do you suppose these people speak?

Questions (5)

1. Talk about Anna.
2. What does she feel about Harry's death?
3. What does Martins now think was strange about Harry's death?
4. Why doesn't Martins like Anna's tea? Do you know how to make a nice cup of tea?

Questions (6)

1. What is Dr Winkler's waiting-room like?
2. Are the bones what they are said to be?
3. How much do you think Dr Winkler knows?

Questions (7)

1. How does Herr Koch receive Martins?
2. What does Herr Koch say about Harry's death?

3. How many people did he see carrying Harry to the house?
4. Why can Herr Koch not describe the people?
5. Who do you think the third man might have been?
6. What happens when Martins speaks of murder?
7. What does the narrator say about Herr Koch's last words? What do you think of this?
8. What does Martins find when he returns to Sacher's?

Questions (8)

1. Where does Cooler live?
2. How did Harry die, according to Cooler? Give the exact words.
3. What does Cooler do when Martins says he thinks there was a third man?
4. How much do you think Cooler knows?
5. Would you trust Cooler?

Questions (9)

1. What does Anna think of Martins coming to see her?
2. What happens between Anna and Martins while they are talking?

3. Does Anna want to fall in love again? Explain.
4. Why do they go to see Koch and his wife?
5. What has happened in the house?
6. What does the child say? Is he right?
7. Why does Anna tell Martins to be carefull?
8. What happens when Martins returns to Sacher's?
9. Where does Martins think the car is going?
10. Where does it in fact go?
11. What is Martins thinking about during the meeting?
12. What kind of books does Martins write, and under what name? (See chapter 2.)
13. Who do the people at the meeting think Martins is?
14. Is it a lie to write "B. Dexter"? Explain.
15. Why does Martins say he wants to go to the toilet?
16. What does Martins think about the sound in the dark room?
17. Buck Dexter is mistaken for Benjamin Dexter. Who else is mistaken for someone else in this chapter?
18. Why does Graham Greene put a parrot in the room, do you think?

Questions (10)

1. Why does Calloway put a wide desk between them?
2. What do you think Cooler could do with the money from his tyre racket?
3. Try to explain the penicillin racket.
4. What deaths has the racket so far caused?
5. Why does Martins look at his hands?
6. How does Calloway show Martins that Lime was a racketeer?
7. What does Martins call the third man?

Questions (11)

1. What time is it when Martins gets to Anna's flat?
2. What does Anna say when Martins says she loves a murderer? What do you think of this?
3. Who does Martins see in the street?

Questions (12)

1. What do you think is the danger to Anna?
2. Why do the International Patrol go to Anna's flat?
3. Talk about the scene in Anna's room.

4. What does the English soldier do while he is outside the door?
5. Where does the Russian want to take Anna?
6. Who stops the car?
7. What happens to Anna?
8. Do you know anyone who has seen a ghost?

Questions (13)

1. Why does Carter want the body dug up?
2. What do the two men find inside the kiosk?
3. What does Martins agree to do?

Questions (14)

1. What does Martins say to Kurtz?
2. Where does Martins want to meet Harry?
3. Who is in Kurtz's other room?
4. How long does Martins wait for Harry Lime?
5. What does Harry say about Anna?
6. What does Martins think about Harry?
7. What does Harry say about the 'little dots'?
8. What does he say about money?
9. What do you think of his ideas of life and death?

10. What does Martins shout after Harry?

Questions (15)

1. What does Anna do when she hears that Harry is still alive?
2. Is Anna going to help to catch Harry? Explain.
3. Was the body in the coffin the one it was said to be?
4. Why is Martins to go and warn Cooler?

Questions (16)

1. What does Martins say to Cooler?
2. Where does Martins wait for Harry Lime?
3. Who else is waiting, and where?
4. What happens when Martins is speaking on the telephone?
5. Try to explain the sentence, "But I suppose it was not Lime . . . it was Harry."
6. Why does Bates go in front of Martins?
7. Who fires the first shot, and what happens?
8. Who fires the second shot, and what happens?
9. Who fires the third shot, and what happens?
10. Where does Martins find Harry?

11. What does Harry say?
12. Who fires the last shot, and what happens?
13. What animal is mentioned in this chapter, and how often - and why, do you think?

Questions (17)

1. What is the weather like now?
2. In what way is the end of the story like a beginning?
3. Now, how about reading this story in the original, as Graham Greene wrote it?